Mallard, Mallard, Moose

Mallard, Mallard, Moose

by Lori Doody

For my grandmother, who loved books

One early morning, just as the sun rose over Signal Hill, a moose came to town.

He wasn't lost. He wasn't looking for food.
He was trying to find a home for two mallard ducks
who were following him everywhere he went.

The moose didn't know why the ducks
liked him; he definitely couldn't
be mistaken for their mother.

It was beginning to put him in a foul mood.

So he tried leaving them at a popular park,

but the ducks were nervous of the swans.

SILVER THAW
JEWELRY

He meandered downtown to see if he could
find them a home there,

but the ducks were uneasy of the pigeons.

He trotted through a charming harbourside
neighbourhood,

but the ducks were afraid
of the seagulls,

not to mention
a menacing chicken.

He crisscrossed all around town, but he just couldn't duck those pesky mallards.

They wouldn't leave him alone.

He even tried asking some ladies
to take the ducks, but they were
no help at all.

The moose plodded up a particularly steep hill in hopes
of tiring them out, but those mallards just waddled along.

No matter where he went, he couldn't find a place
that fit the bill.

He moseyed along and discovered a bakery that might make a good home—

then he remembered that ducks really shouldn't eat bread.

The moose was beginning to give up hope.
There didn't seem to be anywhere in the whole town
where he could leave those mallards.

Eventually he came by a restaurant
with a promising name,

but the menu made them all a little anxious.

Luckily they soon came to a walking trail by a lake
where they met a friendly goose who agreed
to take the mallards under his wing.

The moose's quest was complete;
he had found a home for the ducks
and some peace and quiet for himself.

He headed out of town, and said goodbye
to the duck,
the duck,
and the goose.

Newfoundland and Labrador is home to many, many moose.
They are frequently seen on roadways across the province, and sometimes,
especially in the spring, make their way into towns and neighbourhoods.
Even into St. John's. They travel alone, or sometimes in small groups,
but never with ducks in tow.

From 2002 to 2012, a Graylag Goose lived in St. John's;
he was not native to Newfoundland but seemed to have a happy life
among the ducks and pigeons around Quidi Vidi Lake.
Locals dubbed him Michael the goose, though others called him Barry.
We like to think he'd have been a better companion for two mallards,
and better suited to life in town, than a moose.

Remember not to feed bread to ducks; it doesn't have the right nutrients
for them and it can make their ponds and their lakes grow too much algae.

Lori Doody was born in St. John's, Newfoundland,
and studied printmaking at Sir Wilfred Grenfell College;
she graduated in 1998.
In 2005 she was named Emerging Artist of the Year
by the Newfoundland and Labrador Arts Council.
She lives in St. John's with her husband, their two children and their dog.
She loves to visit the ducks at the lake, but never feeds them bread.
Mallard, Mallard, Moose is her third picture book.
You can see more of Lori's artwork at: www.loridoody.com

This book was designed by Veselina Tomova
of Vis-à-vis Graphics, St. John's Newfoundland and Labrador
and printed by Friesens in Canada.

978-1-927917-16-9

Running the Goat is grateful to Newfoundland and Labrador's Department
of Tourism, Culture, Industry and Innovation for support of its publishing
activities through the province's Publishers Assistance Program.

Newfoundland
Labrador

Running the Goat
Books & Broadsides Inc.
54 Cove Road / General Delivery
Tors Cove, Newfoundland and Labrador A0A 4A0
www.runningthegoat.com